TWO
SPECIAL CARDS

by Sonia O. Lisker and Leigh Dean

Pictures by Sonia O. Lisker

HARCOURT BRACE JOVANOVICH
New York and London

For Fran Nicita,
a librarian who reads children

B C D E F G H I J K

Library of Congress Cataloging in Publication Data

Lisker, Sonia O.
Two special cards.

SUMMARY: Two children try to grow accustomed to their parents' divorce.
[1. Divorce—Fiction] I. Dean, Leigh, joint author. II. Title.
PZ7.L68Tw [E] 75-35609
ISBN 0-15-292222-9

Hazel Cooper looked out of her bedroom window. She wanted to cry.

Her friend Elizabeth came into the front yard.

"Hi," called Elizabeth. "Can you come out and play?"

"No," said Hazel.

"Oh," said Elizabeth. "Why not?"

"Because," said Hazel, "I'm getting a divorce."

"You can't get a DIVORCE!" Elizabeth shouted.

"Shhhh," said Hazel.

"Only people who get married can get a divorce," Elizabeth whispered.

"HA-ZEL! LUNCH!"

"I have to go," said Hazel. "See ya."

Hazel didn't feel much like eating. Meals weren't fun anymore. First, it was too quiet. Then, there were fights. They started over any dumb thing.

"Say when," said Daddy, holding out the coffeepot.

"Half a cup," said Mom.

Daddy poured and poured. Mom pulled her cup away
as she gave Bingo a piece of toast. Daddy kept on pouring.
Hot coffee spilled all over the table.

"STUPID!" yelled Mom.

"I said, 'SAY WHEN'!" yelled Daddy.
"You care more about those dopey
dogs than you care about me!"

"I said, just 'HALF a cup'!" yelled Mom. "Look who's calling the dogs dopey!"

"Woof-woof," barked Bobo. "Yip-yip," barked Bingo.

"Stop, stop, STOP!" screamed Billy.

YELL! YELL! YELL!

Hazel ran out of the kitchen and out to the backyard.

"Hi," said Elizabeth. She was washing the family car.
"Want to help?"

"O.K.," said Hazel, and picked up the hose. "You
know what, Elizabeth?"

"What?" said Elizabeth.

"Getting a divorce stinks," said Hazel.

She turned on the hose. "Everybody yells, yells,
YELLS!" she yelled. "Do your parents yell at each other?"

"Sometimes," said Elizabeth. "But afterward they hug
and kiss each other and make up."

"My mom and dad never hug each other anymore,"
said Hazel.

"HA-ZEL! WATCH BILLY!" Mom called.

Billy toddled down the back porch steps and over to where Hazel and Elizabeth were working.

"Want to wash, too," said Billy. And he grabbed Elizabeth's sweater and plopped it into the bucket of soapy water.

"STUPID!" shouted Hazel, stamping her foot and pushing Billy away from the bucket.

"Now look what you've done!" she yelled.

Billy began to cry. Mom came to the back door. Daddy came to the back door.

"Hazel, come inside this minute," ordered Mom.

"Go up to your room," ordered Daddy.

Hazel went up to her room and cried.

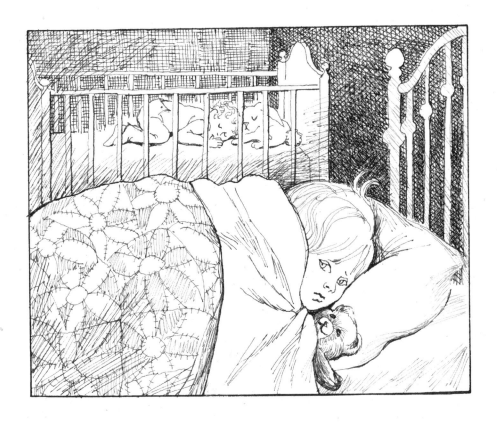

Late that night, Hazel woke up. She heard voices. Loud, angry voices. Mom and Daddy were fighting again. They kept saying the word "divorce." Hazel looked into the crib. Billy was sound asleep. She wished he were older. Then she would have someone to talk to.

Hazel opened the door of their bedroom a crack and peeked down the stairs. Daddy had a suitcase, and he said, "Good-bye. I'll phone the children."

Mom said, "Good-bye." Then she closed the front door and locked it.

Hazel started to feel scared. She went back to bed and hugged her Tillie bear tight. Where was Daddy going this time? Would he come back? Would Mom leave, too? Would she and Billy be left all alone?

Every day Hazel waited for Daddy to come back. The other times Daddy went away, he always came back. But this time he didn't. Whenever she came home from school, Billy was playing as usual, Bobo and Bingo were sleeping, and Mom was writing more magazine stories. Some days, though, Mom just sat at her desk and stared at the typewriter. Hazel wondered: *Does Mom miss Daddy, too?*

One evening, when she and Billy were listening to a story, Hazel asked, "Mom, is Daddy ever coming home?" Mom stopped reading. She looked very serious.

"Daddy isn't going to be living here anymore. You know Daddy and I have been making each other so unhappy for such a long time. We've decided to get a divorce. Everyone will be a lot happier. You'll see." Mom smiled. "You and Billy will live here with me, but you'll spend time with Daddy, too. It'll work out fine, just fine. I love you and Billy very much," Mom said, and she gave Hazel and Billy each a big hug.

One Saturday a truck came. Moving men packed up all
Daddy's things and drove away. Sunday evening Daddy
called. He sounded different. He promised to pick up
Hazel and Billy on Friday after school.

On Friday, Hazel helped pack a small suitcase for her-
self and Billy. She put in pajamas and toothbrushes and
toothpaste and a change of clothes. Billy needed an extra
shopping bag for his Sleep Bunny. Hazel put her Tillie
bear into the bag so Bunny wouldn't be lonely.

At four o'clock Daddy arrived.

"Have a good time," said Mom. "Don't forget to brush your teeth."

"It'll work out fine, just fine," said Daddy.

Everybody waved good-bye.

Daddy had an apartment in the city. Hazel saw lots of
kids in the building for her and Billy to play with. The
elevator ride was smooth. Daddy's place was very clean. It
smelled of pipe smoke.

"We can pretend the plants are a jungle," said Hazel.

"See the big fishes!" said Billy.

"Here's your room," said Daddy, and he opened a door
to a bright red, white, and blue room.

Hazel found pencils and crayons and paper and best of all—bunk beds!

"Can I have the top bunk?" she asked.

"Why not," said Daddy.

"Can we go to bed right after supper?"

Daddy laughed. "I love you Hazel Cooper—and your brother, Billy, too."

That night, Hazel lay awake in her top bunk, thinking how much she loved Daddy and how much she loved Mom. Maybe getting a divorce wouldn't be so bad, after all. Now she and Billy had *two* homes.

For breakfast the next morning, Daddy made his special pancakes shaped like rabbits and ducks. Billy bit off a duck's head. "No more quack," he said. Hazel and Daddy giggled.

After breakfast Daddy looked out of the window. It was raining. "I know a perfect way to spend a rainy day," he said.

"How?" asked Hazel.

"How?" asked Billy.

"I need some pictures to hang on the walls," said Daddy.

All morning Hazel and Billy drew pictures. There must have been fifty when lunchtime came. "They're terrific!" said Daddy, smiling and hugging Billy and Hazel. "I'm going to have a new art show every day till you come back next weekend."

Late Saturday afternoon Daddy brought Hazel and Billy back to the country and kissed them good-bye. Even before Mom opened the front door, they could smell chocolate. Mom had baked a cake and had stuck two candles in the top. Hazel couldn't imagine whom the cake was for. Billy was three and she was almost eight.

"Whose birthday is it, Mom?" she asked.

"Bobo's," said Mom. "Don't you remember?"

Then she said, "Oh no! It's Grandma's birthday, too. I forgot to get a card for Grandma. If we hurry, we can get to the card store before it closes. We'll take stamps along and mail it tonight."

Hazel helped get Billy ready while Mom got the stamps. Mom was always forgetting something. But it was O.K. There were two special cards Hazel wanted to buy.

Mom picked out her cards right away. One said: "Happy Birthday, Mother." And the other said: "Happy Birthday, Grandma," and she let Hazel sign it, "Love from Hazel and Billy." But Hazel couldn't find the kind of cards she wanted. She saw cards about getting engaged and getting married and getting born, but she couldn't find any about getting divorced.

"Hurry up," Mom said. "Bobo can't wait to have his birthday!"

Back home, they all sang "Happy Birthday" to Bobo.

Billy blew out the candles for Bobo, and Mom poured milk for everyone.

"Say 'when,'" she said to Bobo.

"Woof," said Bobo.

After supper, when Billy was tucked in bed with Sleep Bunny and Mom was typing downstairs, Hazel got out the scissors and crayons. She drew a picture of Mom and Daddy together on a big piece of paper. Then she cut the picture apart to make her two special cards.

And she wrote . . .